This book belongs to

_____.

This book was read by

_____

on

_____.

Are you ready to start reading the **StoryPlay** way?

Read the story on its own. Play the activities together as you read!

Ready. Set. Smart!

The BIGGEST Christmas Tree Ever

by Steven Kroll illustrated by Jeni Bassett

CARTWHEEL BOOKS · AN IMPRINT OF SCHOLASTIC INC.

Text copyright © 2009 by Steven Kroll
Illustrations copyright © 2009 by Jeni Bassett
Prompts and activities copyright © 2017 by Scholastic Inc.

Scholastic Inc., 557 Broadway, New York, NY 10012
Scholastic UK Ltd., Euston House, 24 Eversholt Street, London NW1 1DB

Library of Congress Cataloging-in-Publication Data available
ISBN 978-1-338-18735-9

10 9 8 7 6 5 4 3 2 1   17 18 19 20 21
Printed in Panyu, China   137
First edition, October 2017
Book design by Doan Buu

For Kathleen
— S.K.

For Ralph
— J.B.

Once there were two mice who
fell in love with the same Christmas tree,
but you had to see it to believe it.

Do you have a Christmas tree in your house?

Everyone in Mouseville loved Christmas trees.
Every Christmas, families all over town put up the
biggest, most beautiful trees they could find.

But first came Thanksgiving.
The day before the celebration,
Clayton, the house mouse, took a
walk around Mouseville. He knew
he should be thinking about giving
thanks, but the chill in the air
reminded him of Christmas.

"You know what?" he said out
loud. "This year I'm going to find
the biggest Christmas tree ever!"

Not far away, Clayton's friend
Desmond, the field mouse, said
exactly the same thing.

That night, Clayton helped his mom and dad, his brother, Andy, and his sister, Trudy, make a special cheese casserole and a nut pie for Thanksgiving dinner.

Over at Desmond's house, Desmond and his brother, Morris, helped Uncle Vernon fix a big pot of vegetable stew and a cheesecake.

Everyone ate much too much. After dinner, Clayton's grandma and grandpa sat in the living room, holding their tummies and grumbling.

Over at Desmond's, the cousins from across the road stretched out on Uncle Vernon's sofa and took a nap.

Does your family have any Thanksgiving traditions?

The following morning, Clayton woke up early. He wanted to be first at Clara's Christmas Tree Farm at the edge of town. That way, he could have his pick of the biggest trees!

Over at Desmond's house, Desmond tumbled out
of bed with the same thought.

Clayton hurried over to Clara's, but it was hard to go very fast. He was still too full of Thanksgiving dinner. By the time he reached the Christmas tree farm, he was out of breath. He looked around. No one else was there.

Moments later, Desmond arrived. He too was full of Thanksgiving dinner. He too had found it hard to hurry. He took a deep breath and stumbled inside.

Why was it hard for Clayton and Desmond to hurry to the Christmas tree farm?

Clayton wobbled down the rows of trees. Here was a nice one, but it was much too small. There was another, but it was squat and had a crooked top. Over there was a third, but it was average height and had big gaps between the branches.

Struggling down another row, Desmond was having the same problems.

Do you remember what kind of tree Clayton and Desmond are looking for?

Clayton leaned against a tree.
It was scrawny and not very tall.
"I'll never find the tree I want," he said.
"I'd better go home."

And not far away, squinting at another tree, Desmond said, "I'll never find the tree I want. I'd better go home."

Have you ever felt disappointed like Clayton and Desmond felt? What made you feel that way?

When Clayton reached his house, it was only the
middle of the morning. But he was still full, and he
was tired. He fell back into bed.

When Desmond reached *his* house, he too went back to bed.

What do you think Clayton and Desmond will do next? Will they find the perfect Christmas tree?

Clayton woke up for lunch and spoke to his dad.

Dad said, "Go out this afternoon. Walk to the far edge of the Christmas tree farm. The biggest trees are there."

When Desmond woke up for lunch, Uncle Vernon
told him the same thing.

That afternoon, Clayton went out again. At the very same time, Desmond did too.

Clayton walked to the far edge of the Christmas tree farm. He looked at one big tree after another, but none of them looked like the biggest Christmas tree ever.

Down another path, Desmond was having the same bad luck.

This story takes place in the fall. How can you tell? Can you name the other three seasons?

Starting to lose hope, Clayton peered around a very
thick trunk. Desmond peered around the same thick trunk.
They bumped heads and fell down.

"I bet you're looking for the biggest Christmas tree ever!" said Clayton.

"I bet *you're* looking for the biggest Christmas tree ever!" said Desmond.

"Why don't we find it together?" said Clayton.

"No one said we couldn't," said Desmond.

Look at the picture. Which Christmas tree is the biggest? Point to it!

They set out through the rows of trees. They looked and looked until it was almost dark.

Just as they were ready to give up, there it was: a
Christmas tree so big and so tall, it reached the sky!

"How will we cut it down?" Clayton asked. "It's much too big for the two of us."

"Where will we put it?" Desmond added. "It won't fit in your house or mine."

Clayton and Desmond smiled.

"Our families will help us," they said together.

And that is what happened. Clayton's dad and Uncle Vernon came out with their axes, and with the help of Clayton and Desmond, they chopped down the giant tree.

Who would you call if you needed help with something?

Both families called on friends and relations,
and together they loaded the tree onto a hundred red
wagons and pulled it to Clayton's front yard. There
they decorated it with the most wondrous ornaments
and colored lights . . .

. . . and on Christmas Eve, with all of Mouseville celebrating around it, the biggest Christmas tree ever lit up the entire hillside.

Clayton and Desmond shared a high five.

"We did it!" said Clayton.

"All of us together!" said Desmond.

Story time fun never ends with these creative activities!

★ Let's Decorate! ★

Get into the holiday spirit with Desmond and Clayton by making your own paper chain holiday decorations! You will need some colored construction paper, tape or glue, and scissors, plus an adult to help you.

- Have a grown-up help you cut the paper into strips. The more paper you cut up, the longer your chain will be.
- Try using different colored paper to create a pattern.
- Curl a strip of paper into a circle shape, then tape or glue the two ends together.
- Loop the next strip through the first circle you made. Then tape or glue the ends together so it makes another circle.
- Use the rest of your strips to create more circles. Make your chain as long as you would like!

★ A Friendship Story ★

Clayton and Desmond became friends while they were looking for a Christmas tree. Who is your best friend? How did you meet? Draw a picture showing how you and your best friend met for the first time. Then give it to your best friend!